ANGEL™

HUNTING GROUND

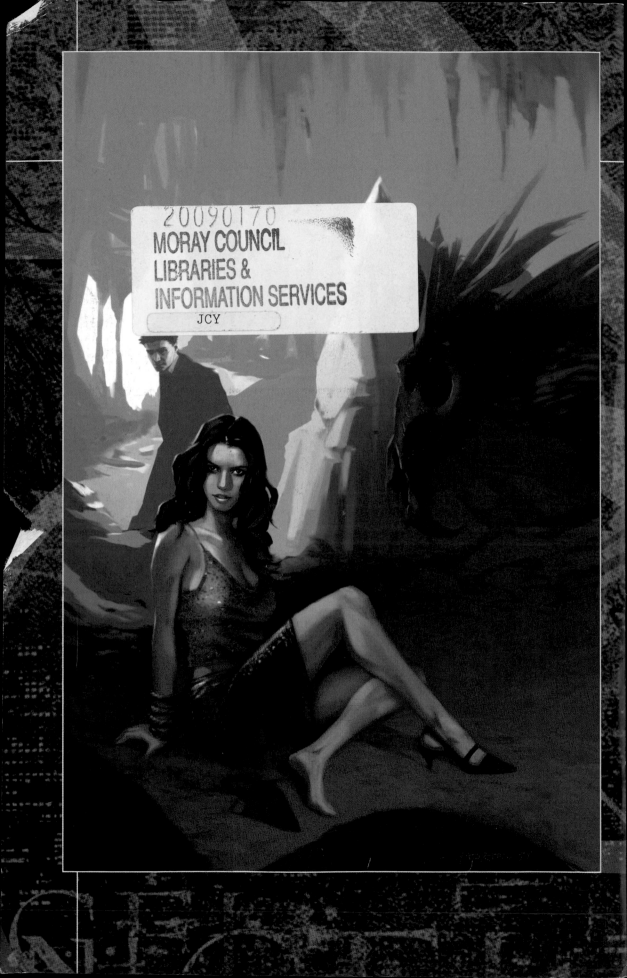

ANGEL ™

HUNTING GROUND

based on the television series
created by
JOSS WHEDON and DAVID GREENWALT

story
CHRISTOPHER GOLDEN and TOM SNIEGOSKI

art
BRIAN HORTON and PAUL LEE

colors
MATT HOLLINGSWORTH

letters
CLEM ROBINS

TITAN BOOKS

publisher
MIKE RICHARDSON

editor
SCOTT ALLIE
with MIKE CARRIGLITTO

collection designer
KEITH WOOD

art director
MARK COX

Special thanks to
DEBBIE OLSHAN at Fox Licensing,
CAROLINE KALLAS and GEORGE SNYDER at
Buffy the Vampire Slayer.

ANGEL: HUNTING GROUND
ISBN: 1 84023 338 9

Published by Titan Books,
a division of Titan Publishing Group Ltd.
144 Southwark St
London SE1 0UP

A CIP catalogue record for this title is available from the British Library.

First edition: October 2001

1 3 5 7 9 10 8 6 4 2

Printed in Italy.
This story takes place during Angel's first season.

What did you think of this book? We love to hear from our readers. Please
email us at: readerfeedback@titanemail.com or write to us at the above address.

IT'S SORT OF A BLAIR WITCH-Y KINDA THING. LOW-BUDGET INDIE HORROR FLICKS ARE ALL THE RAGE. PLUS I'M IN EVERY SCENE, SO I'LL REALLY HAVE A CHANCE TO SHINE.

DON'T WORRY, THOUGH, I'LL COME BACK AND VISIT AFTER I'M FAMOUS.

THE SCRIPT IS A STAR-MAKER, THE KIND OF CHALLENGE EVERY SERIOUS ACTRESS DREAMS OF...THE PRODUCERS TOOK ONE LOOK AT ME, AND I HAD THE PART.

OKAY, THIRD AUDITION, BUT STILL.

CORDELIA CHASE IS BACK ON TOP. I'M TELLING YOU...

"...THIS IS THE BEST THING THAT'S EVER HAPPENED TO ME."

THIS IS A NIGHTMARE. SHOULDN'T I HAVE A BODY DOUBLE FOR THIS STUFF?

YEAH, RIGHT. THEY'RE FEEDING US SLIM JIMS AND POWER BARS AND YOU WANT A BODY DOUBLE. HELL, THEY PROBABLY STOLE THE CAMERAS.

COMPLAIN IF YOU WANT, MAN, BUT I'M JUST GLAD FOR THE OPPORTUNITY. Y'NEVER KNOW, INDEPENDENT MOVIES ARE ALL THE RAGE NOW.

WE SHOULD SHOOT THE LAST SCENE AGAIN. I DIDN'T COME ACROSS SCARED ENOUGH. IT ISN'T EASY WORKING UP A NICE FROTH OF FEAR OVER A PILE OF ROCKS.

YOU WERE FINE. IT'S JUST THE BEGINNING ANYWAY. IF THE PRODUCERS FOLLOW THEIR OUTLINE, THERE'LL BE PLENTY TO BE AFRAID OF LATER.

AND WHAT'S WITH THAT OUTLINE THING? I DIDN'T KNOW THERE'D BE THIS MUCH IMPROVISATION.

IF THEY WANTED US TO COME UP WITH DIALOGUE, THEY SHOULD'VE PAID US GUILD MINIMUM TO WRITE A SCRIPT.

I'M WITH YOU, CORDELIA. IMPROV MAKES IT MORE REAL, BUT I WOULDN'T MIND HAVING A SCRIPT. I DID THIS ONE DEODORANT COMMERCIAL...

HEY, ONE PIECE OF GOOD NEWS. THE GLOBAL POSITIONING SYSTEM IS WORKING. SO WE CAN'T GET LOST.

COOL. WE'LL BREAK CAMP EARLY, AND GET TO THE CAVE BY TOMORROW AFTER- NOON.

IF WE'RE GETTING UP EARLY, WE SHOULD GO OVER TOMORROW'S SCENES TONIGHT. WHAT DO WE HAVE, THE BIG ANTLER DUDE?

GOD, LOOK AT ME. I NEED SLEEP. IF YOU GUYS WOULD WORK FASTER AND TALK LESS, WE MIGHT ALL LOOK HALFWAY DECENT FOR THE CAMERA TOMORROW.

ON THE OTHER HAND, LOOKING AT YOU TWO, MAYBE THAT'S TOO--HEY! WHY'S THERE ONLY ONE TENT?

THIS IS TURNING INTO A NIGHTMARE.

INTRUDERS. TURN BACK. LEAVE THIS PLACE. YOU HAVE BEEN WARNED.

OH GOD.

CASEY, DID YOU HEAR THAT? MAYBE WE SHOULD--

NO WAY, MAN. WE GET TO THAT CAVE TOMORROW, WE GET THE HELM, AND WE GET OUT OF HERE, OR WE DON'T GET PAID.

OOH, I HATE THIS PART!

DON'T BE SUCH A BABY. LIKE YOU HAVEN'T SEEN THIS HAPPEN BEFORE.

I DON'T HEAR ANY-THING.

IT CAME FROM OVER THERE, I SWEAR TO GOD. MAN, HOW LONG 'TIL SUN-UP?

DAVE, CALM DOWN. NOTHING'S GONNA HAPPEN. THERE'S NOTHING OUT THERE.

OH, MAN!

WOW. I DIDN'T THINK THEY HAD THE BUDGET FOR SOMETHING LIKE THAT.

WHAT THE HELL IS THAT?!

OH GOD, OH GOD -- I KNEW THIS WAS A BAD IDEA. "YOU'LL BE THE PRINCESS OF INDEPENDENT FILM," THEY SAID.

LIKE HELL.

MAYBE YOU COULD BE QUIET NOW, SO THEY WON'T *EAT* US?

ALL RIGHT, LISTEN. WE WERE SUPPOSED TO RENDEZVOUS WITH THE CREW AT THAT CAVE IN THE MORNING. THERE MUST BE PEOPLE THERE. IF WE CAN MAKE IT, WE'LL BE SAFE.

HEY, YOU'RE RIGHT. I'VE GOT THE *GPS*. NO WAY CAN WE GET LOST WITH THIS THING. YOU REALLY THINK WE CAN OUTRUN THESE THINGS?

WE HAVE TO.

HOW 'BOUT ANOTHER ROUND?

DEN

THAT WAS THE LAST ONE, ZEKE.

THE HELM OF HARAXIS, TALK.

NOT MUCH TO TELL, REALLY. LOTTA DEMONS DON'T BELIEVE IT EXISTS. IT WAS PART OF THE DEMON ARMOR HARAXIS MADE FOR HIMSELF BACK IN THE 9TH CENTURY.

LEGEND SAYS IT GAVE HIM POWER TO COMMAND OTHER DEMONS. LEASTWAYS 'TIL SOME WHITE HATS KILLED HIM, HID THE HELMET AWAY SOME-WHERES.

"SOMEWHERE AROUND HERE?"

"RUMORS HAVE IT THAT IT CAN BE FOUND SOMEWHERE IN A PATCH OF SEQUOIA NATIONAL PARK NICKNAMED THE WARNING WOOD.

"THE SPIRITS OF THE WOOD GUARD THE HELM TO KEEP IT FROM FALLING INTO THE WRONG HANDS. BUT NOW YOU KNOW WHAT YOU'RE LOOKING FOR, AND WHERE TO FIND IT."

"THE HELM SHOULD BE EASY ENOUGH TO FIND FOR A BRIGHT BOY LIKE YOU.

"THOUGH WHY YOU WANNA GO ALL THAT WAY TO KILL YOURSELF I DON'T UNDERSTAND. YOU WANNA DIE, THERE'S PLENTY MORE FUN WAYS TO DO IT HERE IN L.A."

OH, GOD, I CAN'T TAKE THIS ANY-MORE.

RELAX, WILL YOU?

HE'S A FRIEND.

I DON'T THINK I'VE *EVER* BEEN THIS GLAD TO SEE YOU. AND Y'KNOW THAT WHOLE THING ABOUT MY QUITTING? JUST JOCKEYING FOR A RAISE, HOPING YOU'D COME AFTER ME.

AND HERE YOU ARE. SO, YES, I'LL BE HAPPY TO TAKE MY OLD JOB BACK.

GLAD TO HEAR IT. FIRST, THOUGH, MAYBE WE SHOULD THINK ABOUT--

YOU KILLED IT!

IT'S ONE OF THE SPIRITS OF THE WOOD. THEY CAN'T BE KILLED. ONLY SLOWED DOWN.

THEY THINK WE'RE HERE TO STEAL FROM THEM, AND THEY'LL KILL US ALL TO PREVENT THAT. WE'VE GOT TO GET OUT OF HERE BEFORE--

UM... WHAT'S PLAN B?

YOU READ THE TREATMENT. IT DIDN'T OCCUR TO YOU THAT THE PRODUCERS MIGHT BE DEMONS IN DISGUISE, HOPING YOU'D GET PAST THE FOREST SPIRITS?

HELLO? I'M AN ACTRESS. I WAS HIRED TO PLAY A PART. NOT *EVERY* HOLLYWOOD PRODUCER IS A DEMON.

CAN WE JUST GO NOW? I'LL DEAL WITH THIS CRUSHING BLOW TO MY CAREER LATER.

THEY THINK YOU'RE HERE TO STEAL THE HELM, THEY'RE NOT JUST GOING TO LET US LEAVE.

BUT WE DIDN'T, I MEAN...WE DID, BUT WE WERE JUST ACTING.

TRY TELLING *THEM* THAT.

THEY DID IT! THEY'RE IN THE CAVE!

AAARRGHH!

LOOK, NOBODY WANTS THIS FIGHT. THESE PEOPLE WERE TRICKED INTO COMING HERE. IF YOU LET US GO, WE'LL JUST LEAVE. ONE WAY OR ANOTHER, THOUGH...

...WE'RE LEAVING!

EVEN IF WE HAVE TO GO THROUGH EVERY ONE OF YOU ON THE WAY.

GRRRRRRR!

A VAMPIRE, HUH. WE SHOULD HAVE THOUGHT OF THAT BEFORE.

INTRUDER.

THAT'S ONE POINT OF VIEW. LOOK, THEY DIDN'T COME HERE TO STEAL ANYTHING. THEY WERE DUPED BY A COUPLE OF LOW-LIFE DEMONS WHO--

YOU GUYS JUST DON'T LISTEN.

WHAT ARE YOU TALKING ABOUT? THEY'RE HERE, DON'T YOU GET IT? WE CAN GO HOME NOW. WE'RE GOING TO LIVE. JUST GIVE THEM THE STUPID HELMET, AND--

I DON'T THINK SO. SEE, I READ THE PLOT. OKAY, SKIMMED, BUT JUST NOW, FIGHTING THOSE SPIRITS, I REMEMBERED WHAT THIS STUPID THING IS SUPPOSED TO BE ABLE TO DO.

I KNOW WHY YOU MORONS WANT THIS THING, AND YOU'RE NOT GETTING IT. NOW BACK OFF, AND DON'T MAKE ME USE IT.

SEE WHAT HAPPENS WHEN YOU MESS WITH US? JUST GIVE US WHAT WE WANT, AND WE'LL LET YOU LIVE. LOOK WHAT YOU'RE DEALING WITH, LITTLE GIRL. WE'LL TEAR YOU APART.

KRAKK

ARE YOU KIDDING? I EAT MOOKS LIKE YOU FOR BREAK-FAST...WHEN I'M DIETING.

LIKE I SAID, I READ THE PLOT SUMMARY YOU GUYS WROTE. AND BADLY, DID I MENTION THAT? NOW... FREEZE!

I CAN'T MOVE!

OF COURSE NOT, YOU IDIOT!

THE HELM OF HARAXIS GIVES THE WEARER THE POWER TO COMMAND THE FORCES OF DARKNESS.

THAT'D BE YOU.

"NOW GET OUT THERE AND DISTRACT THOSE SPIRITS SO ANGEL CAN GET OUT OF HERE."

UHNFF!

HEY! HEY! OVER HERE! DON'T KILL HIM, KILL US INSTEAD!

THERE YOU GO. PUT YOUR HEART INTO THE PERFORMANCE. COME ON! I'VE SEEN BETTER ACTING ON *THE MUPPET SHOW*.

THAT'S RIGHT, ANTLER-FACE! WE'RE THE ONES WHO TRIED TO STEAL THE HELM. WHAT OF IT?

I GUESS YOU FIGURED OUT HOW TO USE THE HELM.

INTRUDERS.

WAAAKKK!

THE END

Brian Horton is someone I'd wanted to work with for a long time. We've done a couple of bits and pieces over the years, but the preceding story is to date the biggest project we'd handled. Brian's finishes over Paul Lee can also be seen in *Buffy the Vampire Slayer: The Blood of Carthage*, and their painted work will soon grace a *Buffy* graphic story album, written by the writers of the monthly *Buffy* comic, Tom Fassbender and Jim Pascoe, the infamous boys of Uglytown.

For the original run of this story in *Dark Horse Presents*, Brian made up for the fact that the pages ran in black and white by painting three gorgeous covers. The style was inspired by the original title of the story, "Lovely, Dark, and Deep," which has a distinctly pulpy ring to it.

Brian and I went through a very long and sometimes tedious process of getting these covers just right, and thought it would be of some interest to show it here, in its various phases, for the cover to the second issue of the run.

This first "sketch" will strike people as a pretty strange way to start a painting, with its combination of photographs, sweeping color, and chunky figures. Brian's work is largely done on the computer though, combining figures drawn on paper, drawn on screen, and borrowed from elsewhere. We decided that this image was too passive, and too much like the cover to *DHP* #153 (see page 4 of this volume). Another sketch was needed.

This time Brian skipped the photography, and stuck to brush and ink, which he then scanned and layered with color in Photoshop. This was much more what I was looking for. Next, we needed to get the likeness of Angel approved by David Boreanaz's publicist, so before doing any more work, he painted that face, working it into the composition. Again, this makes for a strange image, but it was a necessary step in the development of the image.

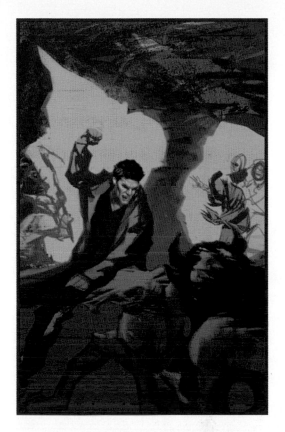

Finally he was ready to finish up the figures, and work Cordelia in. After this, it was just a matter of fine-tuning. The bison man didn't fit with the sorts of creatures described in Golden and Sniegoski's script, so he was deleted, to give more room for other figures. Angel's movement was exaggerated for greater dynamics, and Cordelia was teamed with a member of her film crew. Lighting effects were manipulated to direct the eye and control the composition, until finally Brian arrived at the piece which was recognized in the Society of Illustrators' prestigious *Spectrum Magazine*, #7, in their book section, and can be seen on the following page.

— Scott Stuart Allie

ANGEL ™

BENEATH THE SURFACE

story
CHRISTOPHER GOLDEN
and TOM SNIEGOSKI

art
ERIC POWELL

colors
LEE LOUGHRIDGE

letters
PAT BROSSEAU

Cover by JEFF MATSUDA and JON SIBAL
Colors by GUY MAJOR

DAWN OVER THE CITY OF ANGELS.

ALREADY, THE NEW DAY BEGINS, THE POPULATION STIRRING TO INDUSTRIOUS LIFE...

...EVEN AS THE CREATURES OF THE NIGHT...

...WITHDRAW INTO DEEPER SHADOWS...

THAT'S RIGHT, ANGEL. RUN OFF AND HIDE FROM THE SUN. BUT DON'T GET TOO COMFORTABLE. WON'T BE TOO LONG 'TIL THEY DRAG YOU OUT INTO THE LIGHT OF DAY, AND I'LL BE THERE TO SEE IT.

THE *TIMES* HAS A STORY ON VICTIM NUMBER THREE. THE BODY WAS FOUND NEAR A SEWER OUTFLOW PIPE IN WEST HOLLYWOOD.

I'VE BEEN THERE. A COUPLE OF WEEKS AGO I WAS RUNNING LATE AND HAD TO BEAT THE SUNRISE. IT WAS THE ONLY TUNNEL ENTRANCE CLOSE ENOUGH.

REALLY? WEREN'T THE OTHER TWO BODIES ALSO FOUND NEAR SOME OF YOUR VARIOUS POINTS OF ACCESS TO THE UNDERGROUND?

MUTILATION KILLER'S 3rd VICTIM FOUND

THAT'S RIGHT. WHATEVER'S DOING THIS, I THINK IT'S TRYING TO GET MY ATTENTION.

OKAY, HOLD IT. THIS TRAIN IS OBVIOUSLY HEADED INTO THE CHARITY-WORK STATION, AND WE CAN'T AFFORD TO GO THERE.

I IMAGINE YOU'LL BE DESCENDING INTO THE TUNNELS ONCE AGAIN TO INVESTIGATE. COUNT ME IN!

YOU CAN'T GO OUT IN THE SUN.

BUT YOU'VE BEEN HERE DURING THE DAY.

HOW'S THAT WORK, I WONDER?

SURRENDER, DEMON. YOU DON'T KNOW WHO YOU'RE DEALING WITH.

I ONCE FOUGHT A KULKAS DEMON TO A STANDSTILL WITH NOTHING MORE THAN A POCKET KNIFE, AND I HAD A DEVIL OF A HEAD COLD TO BOOT.

SWAKK

ARRRGH!

BACK OFF. I DON'T LET MY PEOPLE GET HURT. ONCE WAS ENOUGH.

KRACK!

COME BACK HERE, YOU COWARD!

WESLEY! ARE YOU ALL RIGHT?

ASIDE FROM THE BLOOD AND THE EXCRUTIATING PAIN, I BELIEVE SO, YES. I THINK I HAD HIM ON THE ROPES, THOUGH, DON'T YOU?

ABSOLUTELY.

COME ON, LET'S GET YOU PATCHED UP. THEN I WANT TO HAVE ANOTHER TALK WITH OUR NEW FRIEND, ABNER.

SO LET ME GET THIS STRAIGHT. YOUR CATS ARE TRYING TO KILL YOU, AND THEY'VE HIRED CIRCUS CLOWNS TO DO THE JOB? OH, ABSOLUTELY. CIRCUS CLOWNS ARE VERY SCARY.

KNOW WHAT'D BE GOOD? WHY DON'T YOU CALL BACK WHEN THE BOSS IS HERE. JUST ASK FOR ANGEL.

THE PROBLEM WITH THIS JOB IS IT'S TAKEN AWAY MY ABILITY TO JUDGE THE BIZARRE-BUT-TRUE FROM THE COMPLETELY INSANE.

I THINK I KNOW HOW YOU FEEL.

I NEED TO TALK TO HIM.

HE'S OUT ON A CASE. IF YOU WANT TO WAIT, THERE MAY BE A COUPLE OF DONUTS LEFT FROM THIS MORNING.

THIS ISN'T A SOCIAL CALL. WHAT CAN YOU TELL ME ABOUT HIS WHERE-ABOUTS THE NIGHT BEFORE LAST?

DONUTS

I'M SORRY. DID YOU JUST ASK WHAT I THINK YOU ASKED? YOU'RE WAY OFF BASE, DETECTIVE.

I CAN TELL YOU WHERE ANGEL WASN'T LAST NIGHT. THAT'S WHEREVER YOU'RE THINKING HE MAY HAVE BEEN. NOW DON'T YOU HAVE OTHER INNOCENT PEOPLE TO HARASS?

ACTUALLY, I THINK I'LL HAVE A LOOK FOR MYSELF.

YOU CAN OBJECT OF COURSE, BUT THEN I'LL HAVE TO MAKE IT ALL OFFICIAL, AND THAT WOULD DRAW ATTENTION I'M SURE ANGEL DOESN'T WANT.

YOU'RE A ROTTEN, EVIL PERSON. I'M SURE YOUR PARENTS ARE VERY PROUD.

YOU HAVE A STRANGE WAY OF DEFINING EVIL. AND YOU DON'T KNOW ANYTHING ABOUT MY PARENTS.

HEY, PUT THAT DOWN! HE'LL REALLY BE ANNOYED IF YOU LOSE HIS PLACE.

WHERE DOES THIS GO?

STORAGE.

I'M GOING TO HAVE TO ASK YOU TO LEAVE NOW. IF YOU WANT TO CAUSE ANGEL PROBLEMS OVER THAT, I GUESS IT'S UP TO YOU.

BUT GO.

I THINK I FOUND WHAT I WAS LOOKING FOR.

CAREFUL, JIMBO, YOU CAN'T AFFORD TO GET COCKY DOWN HERE.

AND THAT GOES FOR YOU GUYS, TOO. STAY ALERT.

IF IT'S BIGGER THAN A RAT AND IT MOVES--SHOOT IT.

HEY DETECTIVE, YOU SURE YOU WANT TO DO THAT? WE WOULDN'T WANT THE SMELL TO GIVE US AWAY.

STINKS SO BAD DOWN HERE, WHO'D NOTICE?

WAIT A MINUTE, THINK WE GOT SOMETHING HERE.

THEY HURT ABNER. BUT ABNER'S GETTIN' BETTER.

HMMM. HUNGRY.

GROWIN' BOY'S GOTTA EAT.

KRUNCH!

HUH?

ANGEL--
THE BLOOD
ON HIS
MOUTH.

NO! WHY DO YOU WANT TO HURT ABNER? DESTROY MY THINGS?

ABNER DIDN'T DO NOTHING TO YOU!

IT ISN'T ME. IT'S ABOUT THE SEVEN PEOPLE YOU TORE APART.

MIGHT I SUGGEST SOMETHING SHARP?

SNIFF SNIFF

HOLD OFF A MINUTE, WES.

THAT BLOOD ON YOUR MOUTH ISN'T HUMAN, IS IT, ABNER? I CAN SMELL IT. THAT MAY NOT MEAN MUCH, BUT IT BUYS YOU A CHANCE TO TALK. GIVE ME A REASON TO BELIEVE YOU.

NO! STAY BACK! ABNER DIDN'T HURT NO ONE!

HURKK! TOLD YOU, VAMPIRE...

SCHUNNK!

...ABNER DIDN'T HURT NO ONE!

UNGH!

SWAKK!

KRASH!

WHY THEY WANT TO HURT ABNER?

I'VE GOT A BAD FEELING ABOUT THIS, WES. I'M BEGINNING TO THINK MAYBE HE DIDN'T DO IT AFTER ALL.

HOW IS THAT POSSIBLE? WE FOUND THE BODIES-- AND THE BLOOD ON HIS MOUTH. DON'T TELL ME THAT THERE ARE TWO RAVENOUS DEMON BEASTS ROAMING AROUND DOWN THERE.

WHAT SORT OF DEMON HAS PLASTIC FLOWERS IN ITS LAIR?

OR THE WORKS OF SHAKESPEARE.

THEN AGAIN, I'VE SEEN PLENTY OF MONSTERS WITH AN APPRECIATION FOR THE FINER THINGS IN LIFE.

ANGEL...

HEYAAAAHHH!

SORRY, I JUST HAVE A BIT OF A PROBLEM WITH RATS.

DON'T WE ALL.

THAT EXPLAINS THE BLOOD ON HIS MOUTH.

FREEZE!
DON'T EVEN
BLINK!

KATE?

HANDS
BEHIND
YOUR HEADS!
NOW!

DON'T
MAKE THIS
DIFFICULT, ANGEL.
THERE'S BEEN
ENOUGH KILL-
ING.

WESLEY. WAIT.

YOU'VE KILLED A LOT OF PEOPLE, CLIVE. I'M NOT LETTING YOU WALK AWAY FROM THAT.

WHAT MAKES YOU THINK YOU CAN SAVE THE LADY COP? YOU COULDN'T KEEP YOUR BUDDY DOYLE ALIVE.

I WAS KINDA ANGRY, T'TELL THE TRUTH. HE DIED BEFORE I COULD GET EVEN. YOU AND DOYLE MADE A FOOL OUTTA ME. BUT YOU'RE STILL HERE.

YOU'RE SAYING YOU KILLED THOSE PEOPLE, SET IT UP SO THE COPS WOULD THINK IT WAS ME, JUST BECAUSE I GAVE YOU A BEATING?

GUYS LIKE ME, WE LIVE AND DIE BY THE WORD ON THE STREET. NO WAY I COULD SURVIVE OUT THERE IF I LET YOU GET AWAY WITH WHAT YOU DID.

THIS WAY I GET TO TAKE YOU DOWN, GET MY STREET CRED BACK, AND THE POLICE BLAME YOU. KILLING ALL THE COPS? THAT'S JUST A BONUS.

SHLLRP!

LOOK FOR THESE BUFFY THE VAMPIRE SLAYER TRADE PAPERBACKS FROM TITAN BOOKS.

The Dust Waltz
Brereton • Gomez • Florea
80-page color paperback
ISBN: 1-84023-057-6 **£7.99**

The Remaining Sunlight
Watson • Bennett • Ketcham
80-page color trde paperback
ISBN: 1-84023-078-9 **£7.99**

The Origin
Golden • Brereton • Bennett • Ketcham
80-page color paperback
ISBN: 1-84023-105-X **£7.99**

Uninvited Guests
Watson • Gomez • Florea
104-page color paperback
ISBN: 1-84023-140-8 **£8.99**

Supernatural Defense Kit
Watson • Richards • Pimentel
30-page color hard cover
comes with golden-colored cross,
"claddagh" ring, and vial of "Holy water"
ISBN: 1-84023-165-3 **£19.99**

Bad Blood
Watson • Bennett • Ketcham
88-page color paperback
ISBN: 1-84023-179-3 **£8.99**

Crash Test Demons
Watson • Richards • Pimentel
88-page color paperback
ISBN: 1-84023-199-8 **£8.99**

Angel: The Hollower
Golden • Gomez • Florea
88-page color paperback
ISBN: 1-84023-163-7 **£8.99**

Coming Soon!
Ring of Fire
Petrie • Sook
80-page color paperback
ISBN: 1-84023-200-5

**All publications are available through most good bookshops or direct
from our mail order service at Titan Books.** For a free graphic-novels
catalogue or to order, telephone 01536 764646 with your credit-card details
or contact Titan Books Mail Order, Unit 6, Pipewell Road Industrial Estate,
Desborough, Kettering, Northants, NN14 2SW, quoting reference AHG/GN

OTHER TITLES
AVAILABLE FROM TITAN BOOKS

ALIENS
LABYRINTH
Woodring • Plunkett
136-page color paperback
ISBN: 1-85286-844-9
NIGHTMARE ASYLUM
(formerly Aliens: Book Two)
Verheiden • Beauvais
112-page color paperback
ISBN: 1-85286-765-5
OUTBREAK
(formerly Aliens: Book One)
Verheiden • Nelson
168-page color paperback
ISBN: 1-85286-756-6
ALIENS VS PREDATOR
ALIENS VS PREDATOR
Stradley • Norwood • Warner
176-page color paperback
ISBN: 1-85286-413-3
*THE DEADLIEST
OF THE SPECIES*
Claremont • Guice • Barreto
320-page color paperback
ISBN: 1-85286-953-4
WAR
Various
200-page color paperback
ISBN: 1-85286-703-5
ETERNAL
Edginton • Maleev
88-page color paperback
ISBN: 1-84023-111-4
*ALIENS VS. PREDATOR
VS. TERMINATOR*
Schultz • Ruby • Ivy
96-page color paperback
ISBN: 1-84023-313-3
ANGEL
THE HOLLOWER
Golden • Gomez • Florea
88-page color paperback
ISBN: 1-84023-163-7
SURROGATES
Golden •Zanier •
Owens • Gomez
80-page color paperback
ISBN: 1-84023-234-X
**BUFFY THE VAMPIRE SLAY-
ER**
THE DUST WALTZ
Brereton • Gomez
80-page color paperback
ISBN: 1-84023-057-6
THE REMAINING SUNLIGHT
Watson • Van Meter •
Bennett • Ross
88-page color paperback
ISBN: 1-84023-078-9
THE ORIGIN
Golden • Brereton •
Bennett • Ketcham
80-page color paperback
ISBN: 1-84023-105-X
RING OF FIRE
Petrie • Sook
80-page color paperback
ISBN: 1-84023-200-5
UNINVITED GUESTS
Watson • Brereton •
Gomez • Florea
96-page color paperback

ISBN: 1-84023-140-8
BAD BLOOD
Watson • Bennett • Ketcham
88-page color paperback
ISBN: 1-84023-179-3
CRASH TEST DEMONS
Watson • Richards • Pimentel
88-page color paperback
ISBN: 1-84023-199-8
PALE REFLECTIONS
Watson • Richards • Pimentel
96-page color paperback
ISBN: 1-84023-236-6
THE BLOOD OF CARTHAGE
Golden • Richards • Pimentel
128-page color paperback
ISBN: 1-84023-281-1
STAR WARS
*BOBA FETT: ENEMY OF
THE EMPIRE*
Wagner • Gibson • Nadeau
112-page color paperback
ISBN: 1-84023-125-4
BOUNTY HUNTERS
Stradley • Truman • Schultz •
Mangels •Nadeau • Rubi • Saltares
112-page color paperback
ISBN: 1-84023-238-2
CHEWBACCA
Macan • Various
96-page color paperback
ISBN: 1-84023-274-9
CRIMSON EMPIRE
Richardson • Stradley •
Gulacy • Russell
160-page color paperback
ISBN: 1-84023-006-1
CRIMSON EMPIRE II
Richardson • Stradley •
Gulacy • Emberlin
160-page color paperback
ISBN: 1-84023-126-2
DARK EMPIRE
Veitch • Kennedy
184-page color paperback
ISBN: 1-84023-098-3
DARK EMPIRE II
Veitch • Kennedy
168-page color paperback
ISBN: 1-84023-099-1
*EPISODE I
THE PHANTOM MENACE*
Gilroy • Damaggio • Williamson
112-page color paperback
ISBN: 1-84023-025-8
EPISODE I ADVENTURES
152-page color paperback
ISBN: 1-84023-177-7
JEDI ACADEMY – LEVIATHAN
Anderson • Carrasco • Heike
96-page color paperback
ISBN: 1-84023-138-6
THE LAST COMMAND
Baron • Biukovic • Shanower
144-page color paperback
ISBN: 1-84023-007-X
*MARA JADE:
BY THE EMPEROR'S HAND*
Zahn • Stackpole • Ezquerra
144-page color paperback
ISBN: 1-84023-011-8

PRELUDE TO REBELLION
Strnad • Winn • Jones
144-page color paperback
ISBN: 1-84023-139-4
SHADOWS OF THE EMPIRE
Wagner • Plunkett • Russell
160-page color paperback
ISBN: 1-84023-009-6
*SHADOWS OF THE EMPIRE:
EVOLUTION*
Perry • Randall • Simmons
120-page color paperback
ISBN: 1-84023-135-1
*TALES OF THE JEDI:
DARK LORDS OF THE SITH*
Veitch • Anderson • Gossett
160-page color paperback
ISBN: 1-84023-129-7
*TALES OF THE JEDI:
FALL OF THE SITH*
Anderson • Heike • Carrasco, Jr.
136-page color paperback
ISBN: 1-84023-012-6
*TALES OF THE JEDI: THE
GOLDEN AGE OF THE SITH*
Anderson • Gossett •
Carrasco • Heike
144-page color paperback
ISBN: 1-84023-000-2
*TALES OF THE JEDI:
THE SITH WAR*
152-page color paperback
ISBN: 1-84023-130-0
UNION
Stackpole • Teranishi • Chuckry
96-page color paperback
ISBN: 1-84023-233-1
VADER'S QUEST
Macan • Gibbons • McKie
96-page color paperback
ISBN: 1-84023-149-1
*X-WING ROGUE SQUADRON:
THE WARRIOR PRINCESS*
Stackpole • Tolson •
Nadeau • Ensign
96-page color paperback
ISBN: 1-85286-997-6
*X-WING ROGUE SQUADRON:
REQUIEM FOR A ROGUE*
Stackpole • Strnad • Erskine
112-page color paperback
ISBN: 1-84023-026-6
*X-WING ROGUE SQUADRON:
IN THE EMPIRE'S SERVICE*
Stackpole • Nadeau • Ensign
96-page color paperback
ISBN: 1-84023-008-8
*X-WING ROGUE SQUADRON:
BLOOD AND HONOR*
Stackpole • Crespo •
Hall • Johnson
96-page color paperback
ISBN: 1-84023-010-X
*X-WING ROGUE SQUADRON:
MASQUERADE*
Stackpole •Johnson • Martin
96-page color paperback
ISBN: 1-84023-201-3
*X-WING ROGUE SQUADRON:
MANDATORY RETIREMENT*
Stackpole • Crespo • Nadeau
96-page color paperback
ISBN: 1-84023-239-0

All publications are available through most good bookshops or
direct from our mail-order service at Titan Books. For a free
graphic-novels catalogue or to order, telephone 01536 764 646
with your credit-card details or contact Titan Books Mail Order,
Unit 6 Pipewell Industrial Estate, Desborough, Kettering,Northants,
NN14 2SW, quoting reference AHG/GN.